Costumes on Show

AF604901

Heather Hammonds

CONTENTS

CHAPTER 1

Dressing Up

Do you like to wear dress-ups?
Dressing up can be lots of fun.

Dress-ups are also called **costumes**.
People wear special costumes
when they act in **plays**, **movies** or other shows.

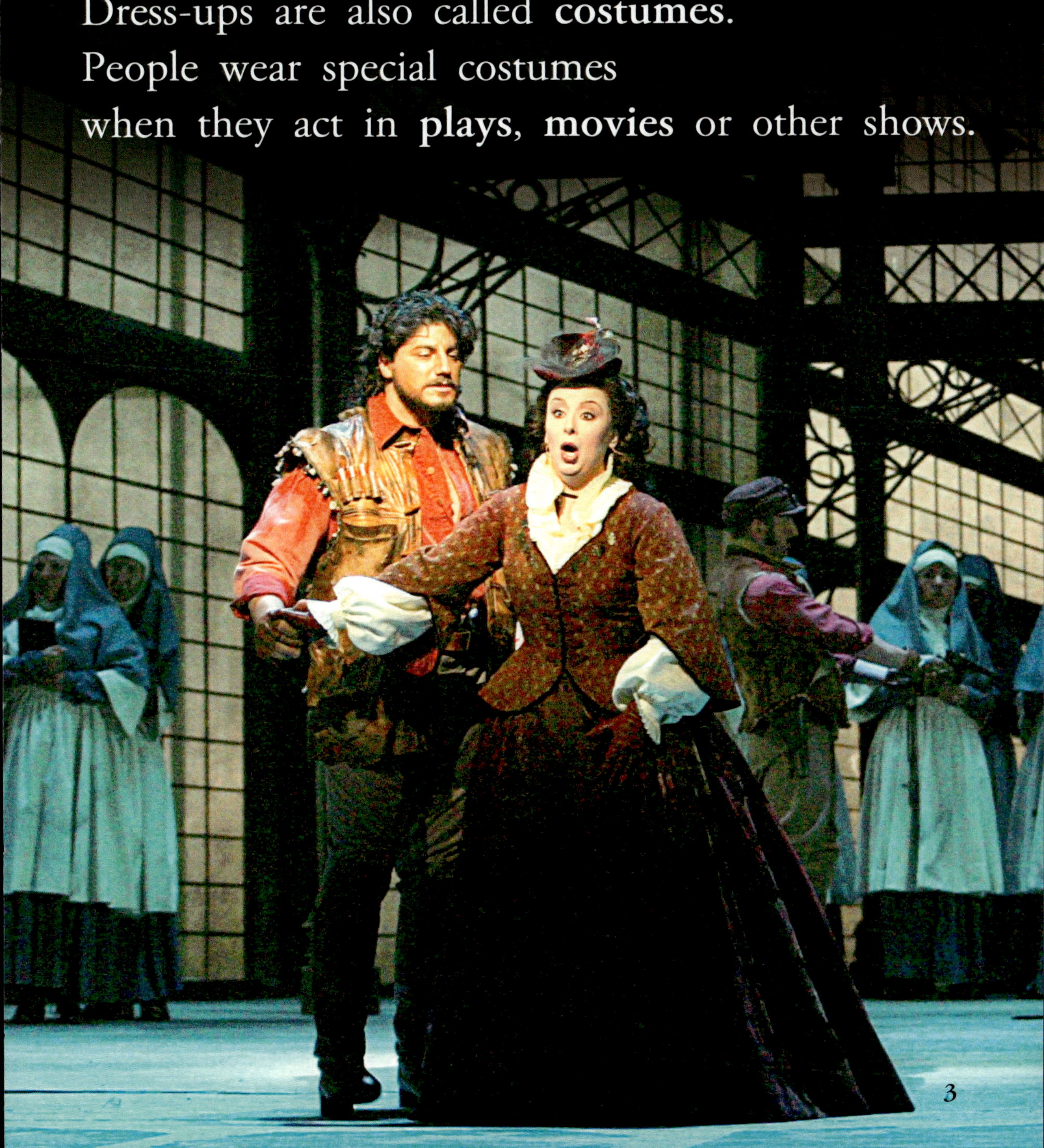

CHAPTER 2

Telling a Story

Costumes help **actors** to tell a story in plays, movies or other shows.

There are lots of children in this show.

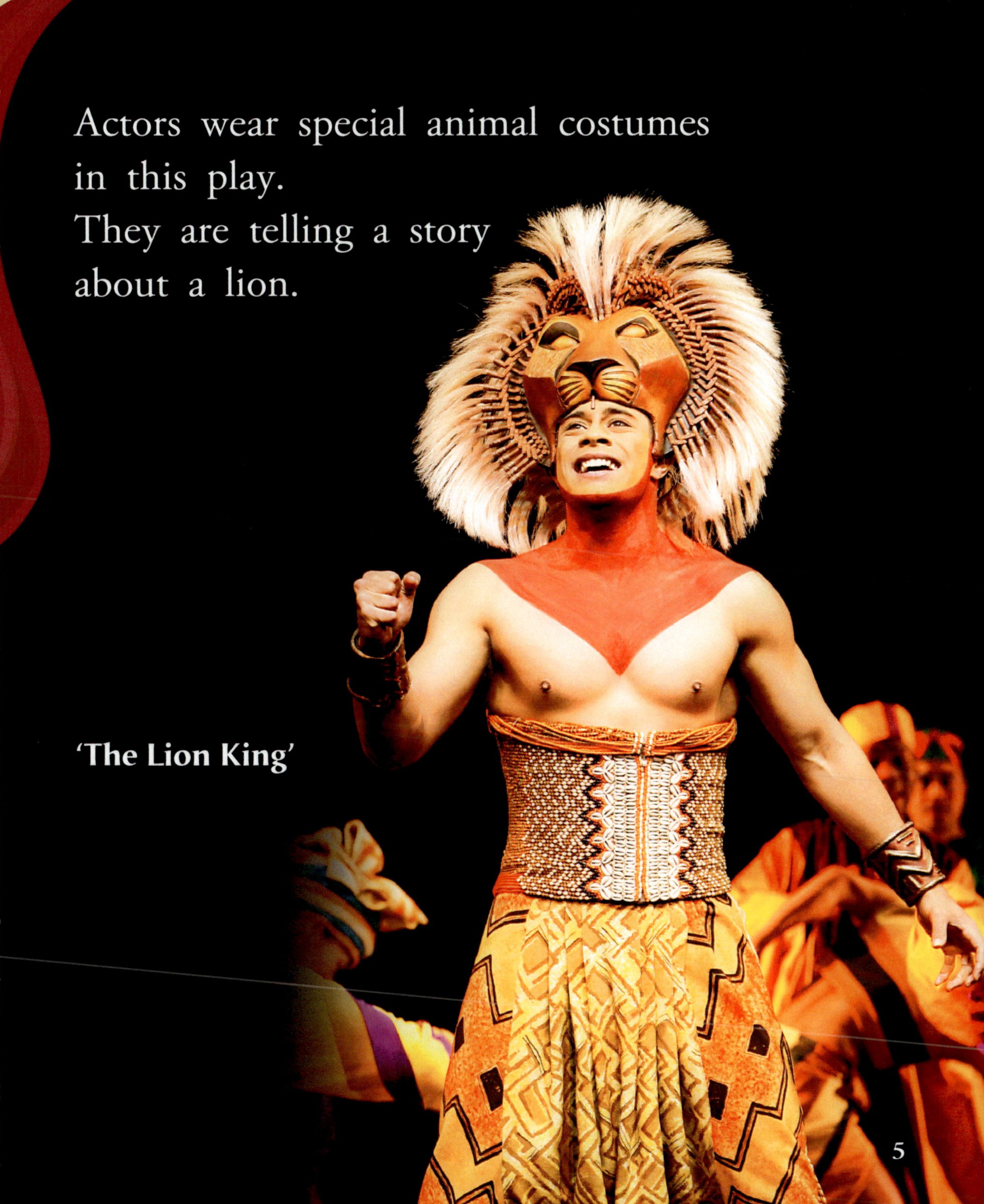

Actors wear special animal costumes in this play.
They are telling a story about a lion.

'The Lion King'

CHAPTER 3

Dance Costumes

Dancers wear costumes to help them look good or tell a story.

Dance costumes are made so that dancers can:

spin…

and bend…

and jump!

These dancers are dressed as birds.
Look at the feathers on their costumes.

These dancers are dressed as cats.
They have very long tails.

These dancers are telling a story about a turtle. Look at their beautiful costumes.

These dancers look like workmen. They are **tap-dancing**.

CHAPTER 4

Costumes from Long Ago

Some plays, movies or other shows tell stories from long ago. Costumes help tell these stories.

This actor is dressed
as a king.
He is in a play
that is very old.

This singer is dressed as a queen.
She is singing in a very old **opera**.

CHAPTER 5

Costumes on Ice

It is fun to go to an ice show. The **ice skaters** in the shows dress in special costumes.

Ice skating costumes are made
so the skaters can spin and jump on the ice.

CHAPTER 6

At the Movies

Movies tell lots of good stories. Costumes help actors to tell a story in movies too.

Some costumes have lots of **decorations** on them. Can you see all the beads?

Some costumes are very scary.

Look at this costume.

We cannot see the actor inside this costume.

This actor has glasses as part of his costume.

CHAPTER 7

Circus Costumes

There are lots of costumes in this show. The costumes look very good!

The **ringmaster** has a special costume.

Clowns put on funny costumes.

Look at this beautiful costume.

CHAPTER 8

Costumes Around the World

People around the world
put on many kinds of costumes.

These costumes are part of a special dance.

dancers from Scotland

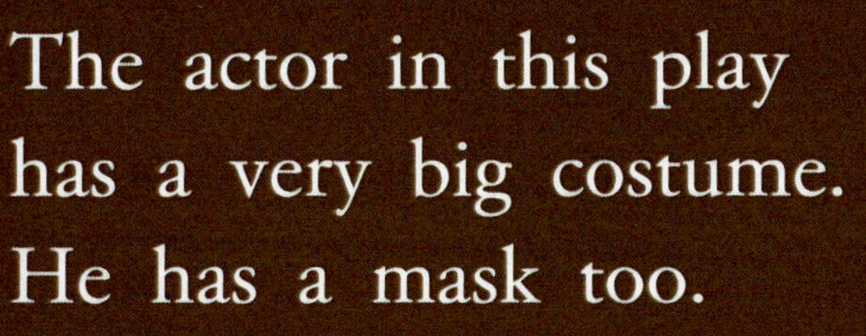

The actor in this play has a very big costume. He has a mask too.

a costume from Japan

These dancers put on paint as part of their costumes.

costumes from Australia

CHAPTER 9

Making Costumes

Making costumes for a play or show takes lots of work.

Actors may need more than one costume. Some costumes take a long time to make.

This is how a costume is made.

reading about the show

drawing the costumes

making the costumes

costumes on show

Glossary

actors	people who act in plays, movies or other shows
costumes	special clothes actors wear in plays, movies or other shows
decorations	things that look good
ice skaters	people who skate on ice
movies	stories told on television or at the cinema
opera	a musical show where actors tell a story by singing
plays	stories told by actors on a stage
ringmaster	the person in a circus who is in charge of the show
tap-dancing	a kind of dancing, where dancers tap their feet as they dance

Index